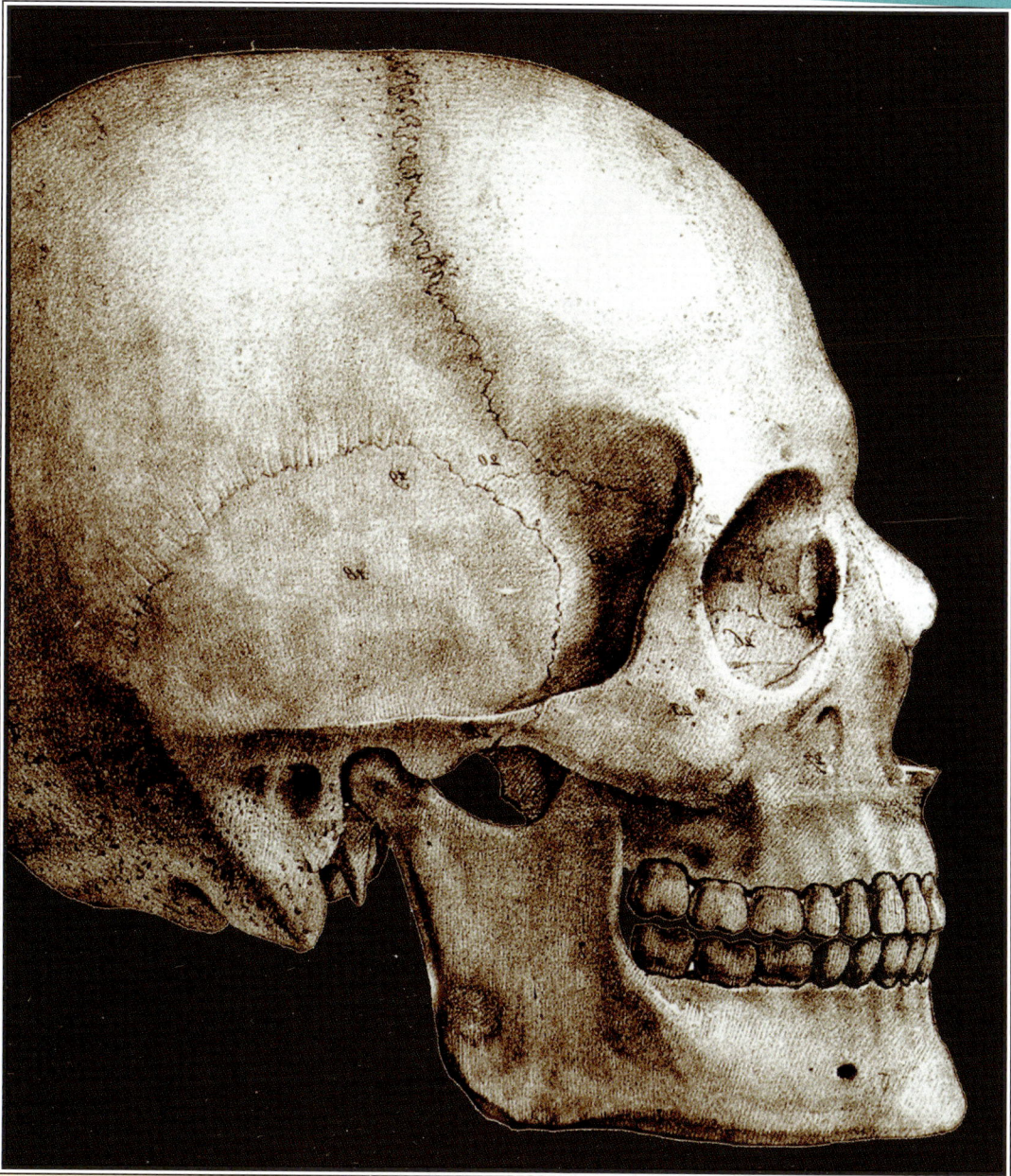

The bones of the skull help to protect the brain

HUMAN BODY

THE $\mathcal{S}$keletal $\mathcal{S}$ystem

Teresa Domnauer

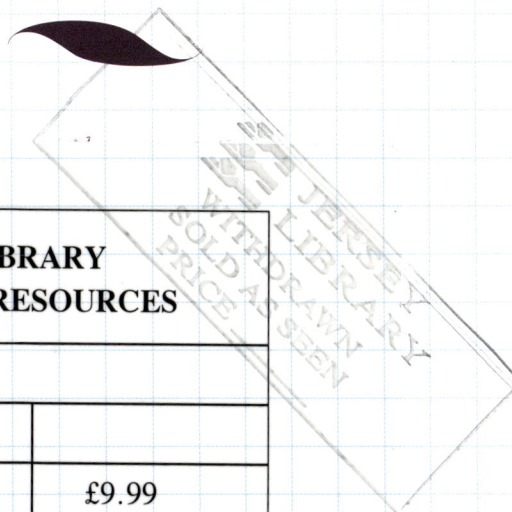

A⁺
Smart Apple Media

COPYRIGHT

Published by Smart Apple Media

1980 Lookout Drive, North Mankato, MN 56003

Designed by Rita Marshall

Copyright © 2004 Smart Apple Media. International copyright reserved in

all countries. No part of this book may be reproduced in any form without

written permission from the publisher.

Printed in the United States of America

Pictures by Corbis (Reuters NewMedia), Custom Medical Stock

Photography (M. Kalab), Digital Vision, Science Photo Library (Prof. P. Motta

(Dept. of Anatomy, University La Sapienza, Rome), Dr. Gopal Murti),

skjoldphotographs.com, Steven Wong

Library of Congress Cataloging-in-Publication Data

Domnauer, Teresa A. The skeletal system / by Teresa A. Domnauer.

p. cm. — (The human body) Includes bibliographical references and index.

Summary: An introduction to the human skeletal system.

ISBN 1-58340-311-6

1. Human skeleton—Juvenile literature. [1. Skeleton. 2. Bones.] I. Title.

II. Human body systems (Mankato, Minn.).

QM101 .D664 2003   611—dc21   2002030904

First Edition 9 8 7 6 5 4 3 2 1

THE Skeletal System

CONTENTS

The Body's Framework

The human skeletal system is made up of 206 connected bones called the skeleton. Skeletons give our bodies shape and structure. They allow us to stand and to move our bodies in many different ways. Without skeletons, we could not walk, run, jump, dance, or do somersaults. We would be shapeless, like lumps of pizza dough! ◥ In addition to giving form to our bodies, bones do many other important jobs. One of their main jobs is to protect **organs**. The skull bones protect

The rib cage bones protect the heart and lungs

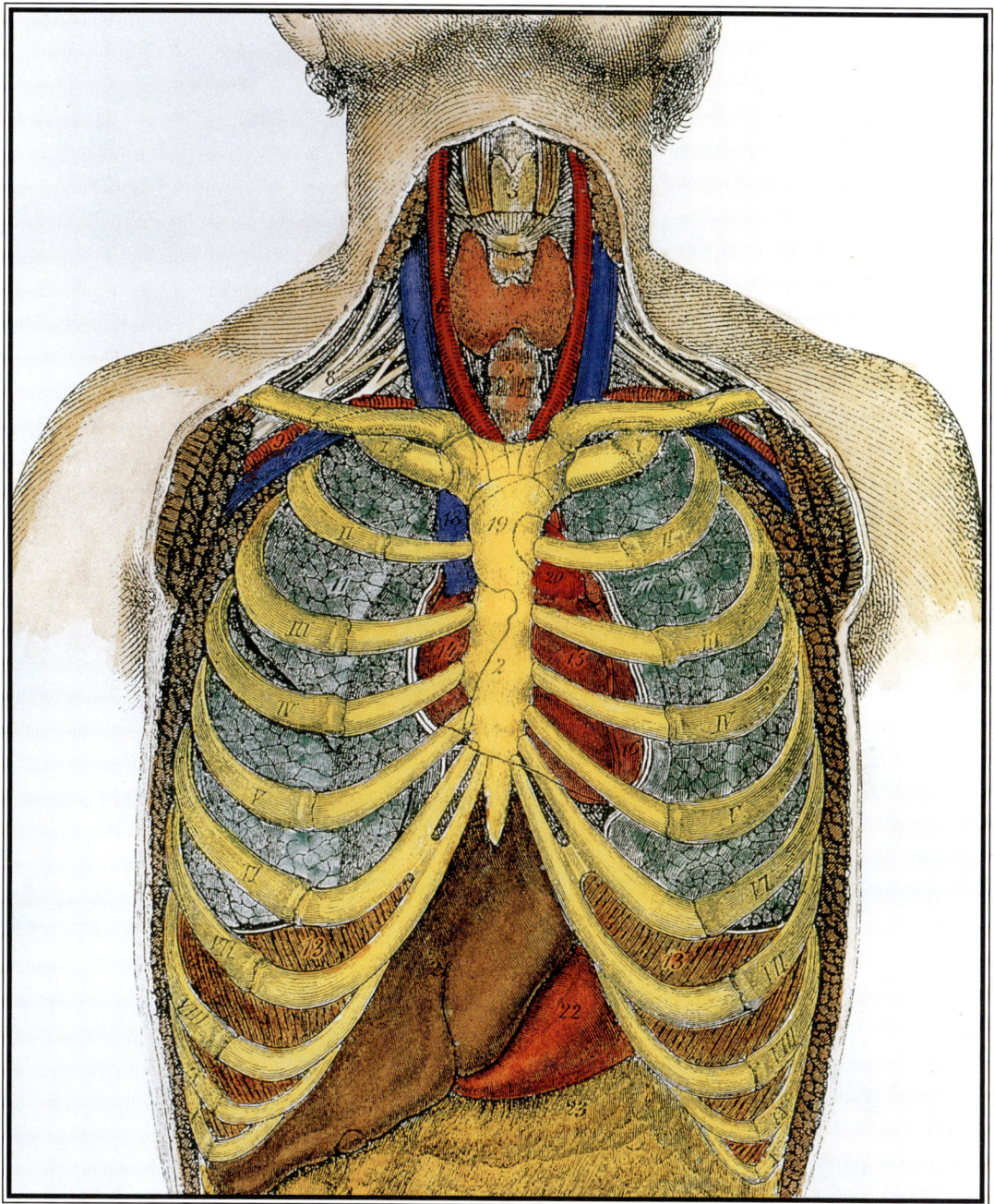

the brain, eyes, and ears. The flat bones of the rib cage protect

the heart, lungs, stomach, and other organs inside our bodies.

The spine protects the **spinal cord**. Bones also make

blood **cells**. Some blood cells are red,

and some are white. Red blood cells

bring **oxygen** to all parts of the body.

White blood cells help keep us from

getting sick.

The smallest bones in the body are found in the ears. The largest bone in the body is the thighbone, called the femur.

This is an up-close look at white blood cells

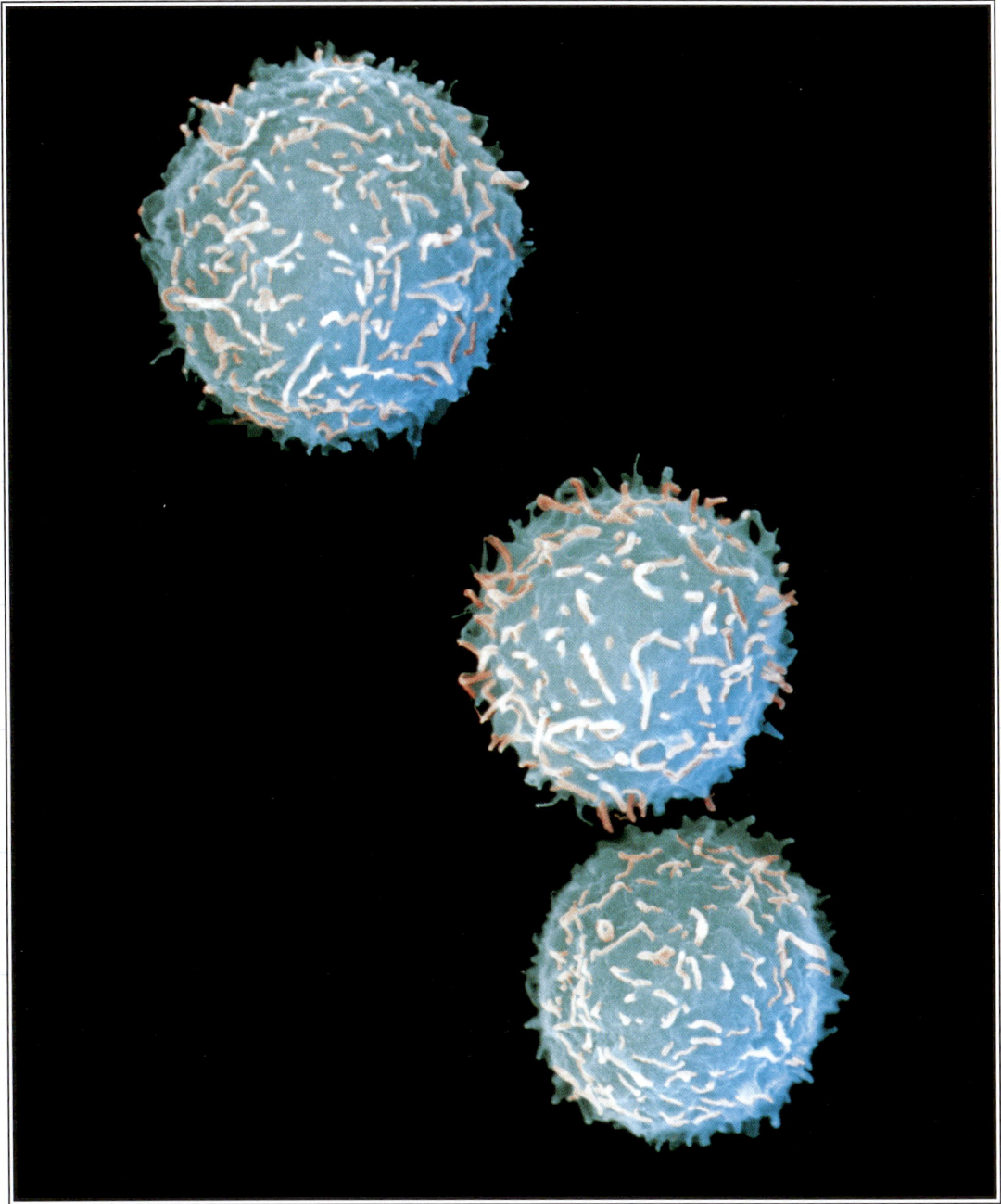

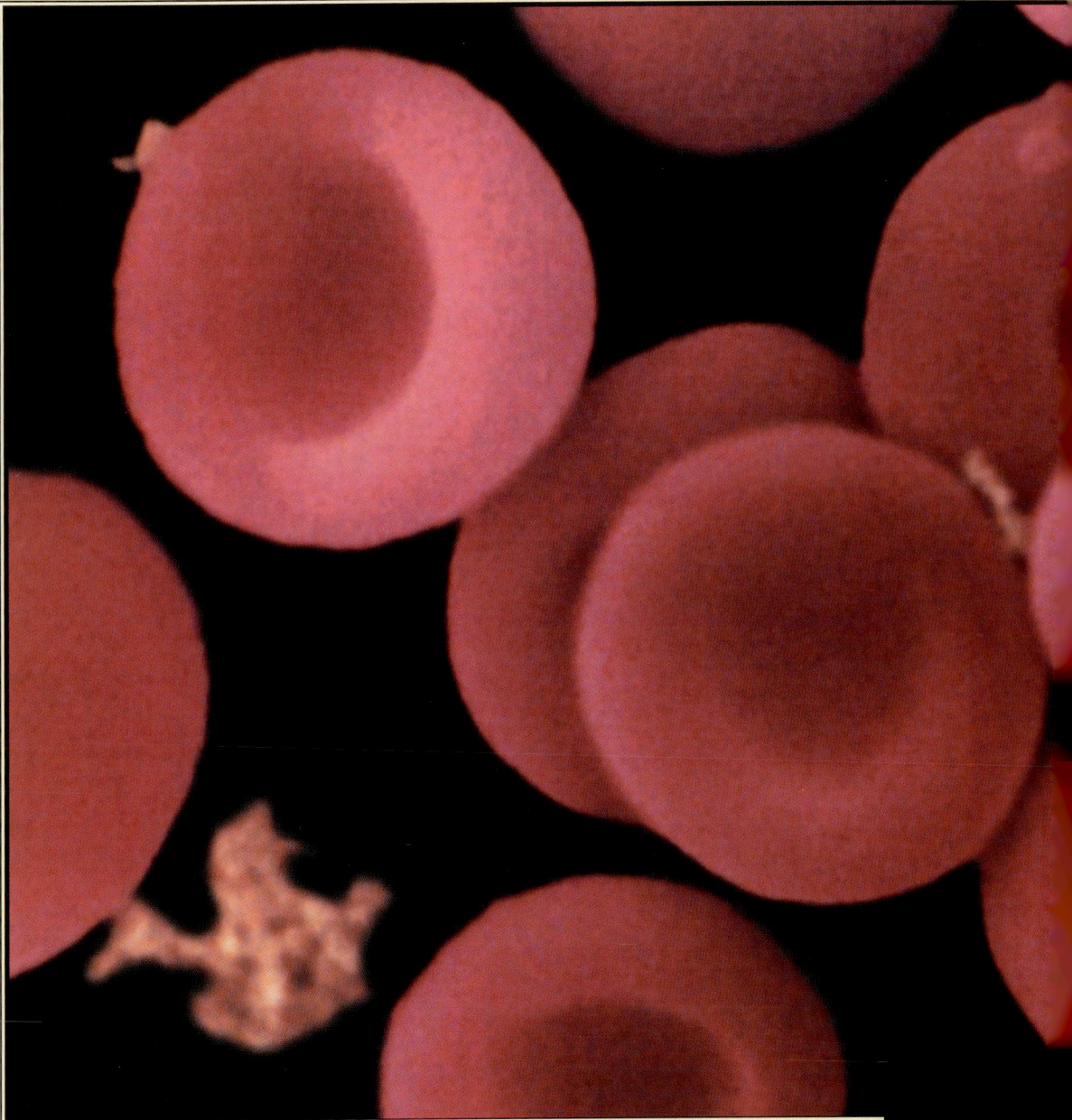

Red blood cells give us energy by carrying oxygen

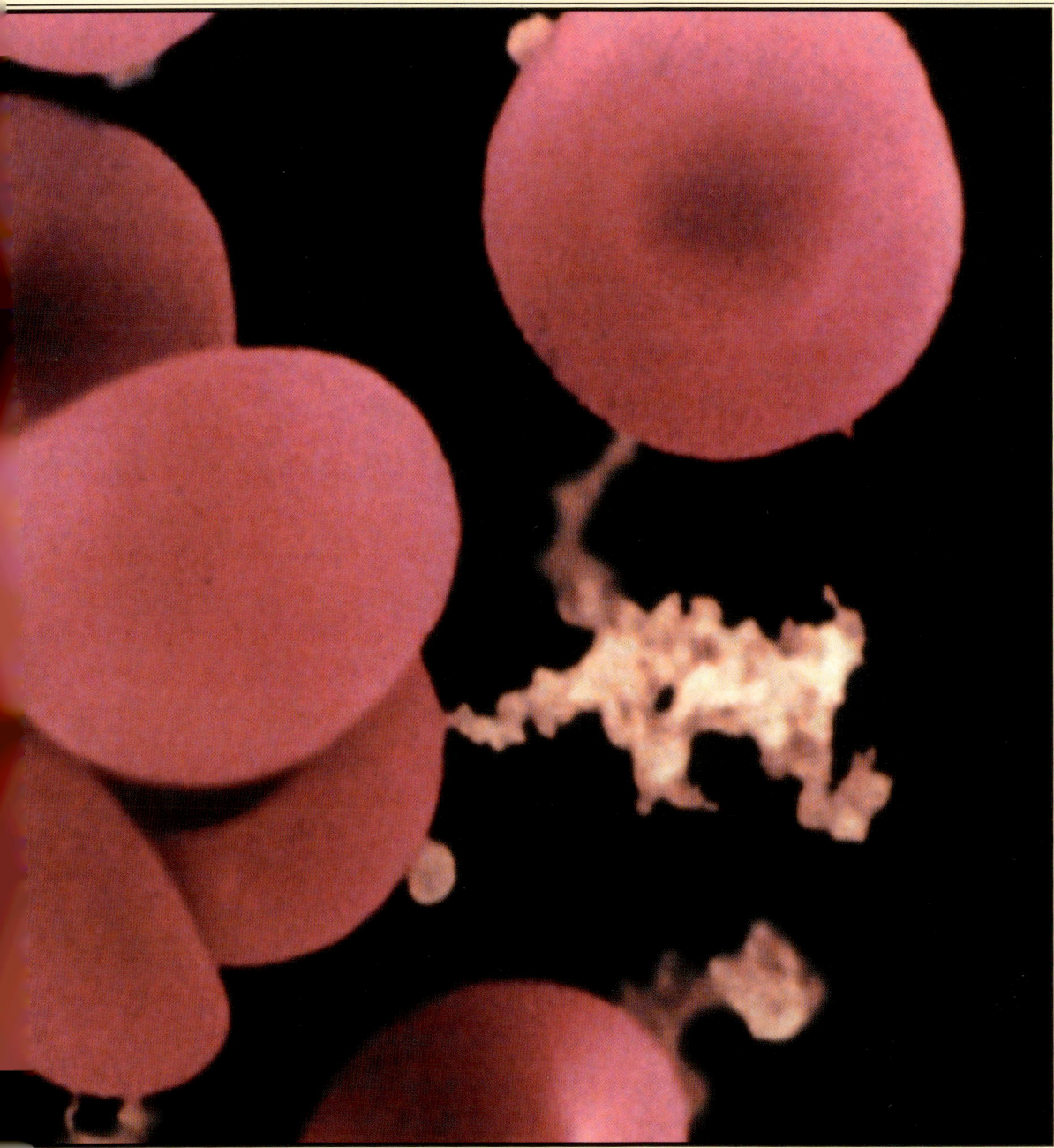

Living Bones

The bony skeleton decorations we see at Halloween may look dead, but the skeletons inside our bodies are full of life. Blood flows through bones, and bones are always growing and changing to meet our bodies' needs. Bones are made of cells and collagen. Collagen is a tough substance woven through our bones that makes them stronger.

The bones in the spine are called vertebrae. There are 33 vertebrae in the spine.

Bones have several layers. The hard outer layer is called compact bone. This layer protects the softer layers of bone

underneath. Spongy bone, found beneath the compact bone,

has tiny holes in it, like a sponge. Some bones have yet another

inner layer called bone marrow. Bone marrow looks like jelly,

This is how bone marrow looks through a microscope

and it produces most of our blood cells. These layers make our bones light but very strong.

Movement

A joint is a place where two or more bones come together. There are several different kinds of joints in the body. The joints in our upper arms and legs allow for a very wide range of movement. Hinge joints, found in our knees, elbows, and knuckles, allow bending movement in only one direction. Some joints do not provide any movement at all, such as the joints where the skull bones meet. ➤ The skeletal

system works with the brain and muscles to move parts of our

bodies. The brain sends messages to the muscles to tell them

how to move. The muscles are attached to bones by tendons,

Muscles push and pull your bones when you move

which are like strong, fibrous cords. When the muscles move,

the bones move, too.

Healthy Bones

Bones are made mostly of calcium. Calcium is a sub-

stance that makes our bones strong and hard. That is why it is

important to eat and drink foods that have lots of calcium.

Milk has a lot of calcium. So does cheese, yogurt, beans, and

spinach. ◣ Exercise is also an important part of keeping

bones healthy. Without regular exercise, bones become softer

Drinking milk helps to build strong, hard bones

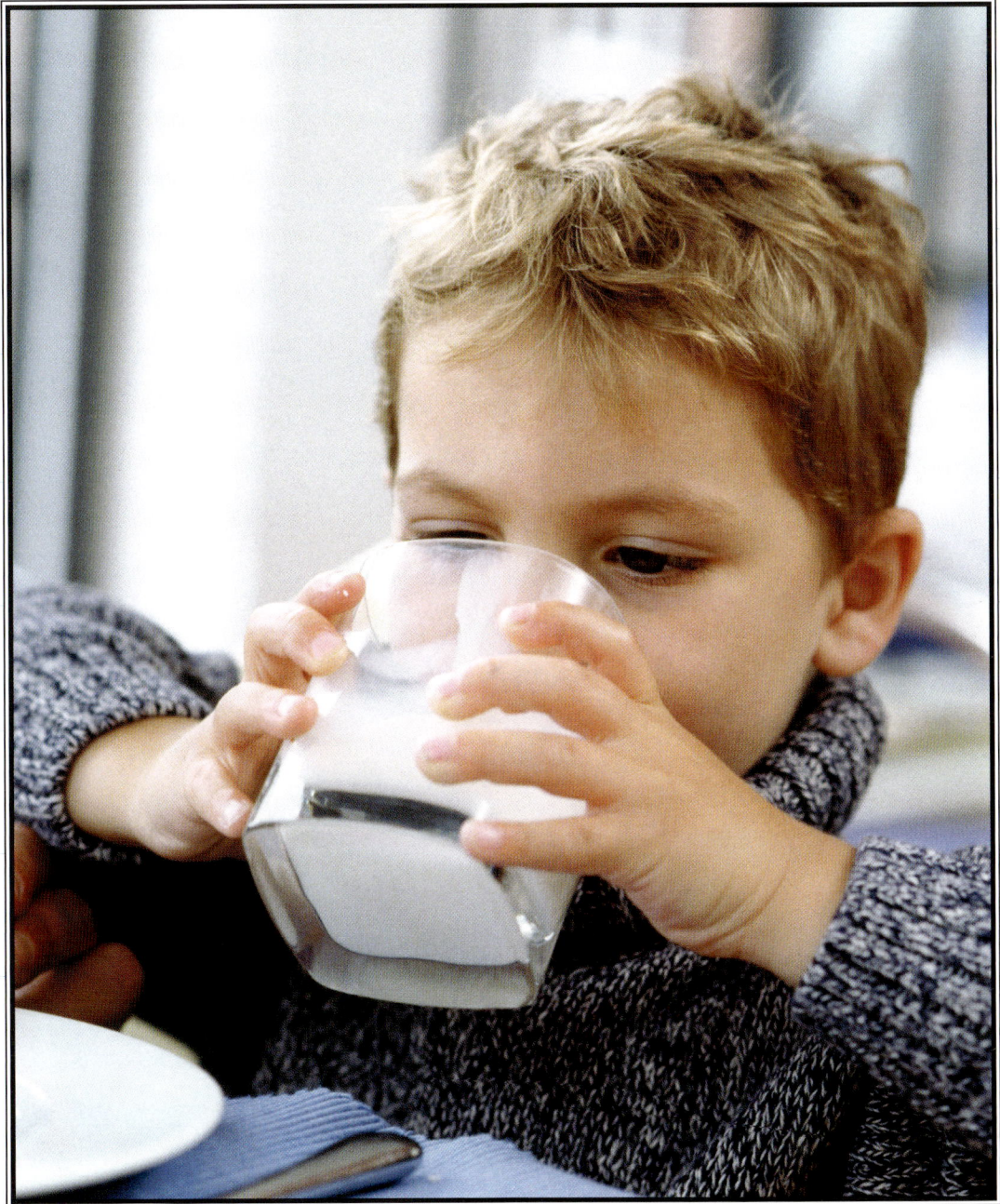

and weaker. Playing sports and being physically active makes

bones harder and stronger. Exercise also energizes the cells

in bones and helps them grow. Even though our bones

are very strong, they can break. But bones **The ankle and knee joints are especially strong because they carry most of a person's weight.**

have the amazing ability to heal by them-

selves. The minute a bone breaks, special

cells in the bone start the healing process

by forming a **blood clot**. Sometimes a doctor will need to

reset a broken bone in order to put the bone parts back where

These are X-ray pictures of broken leg bones

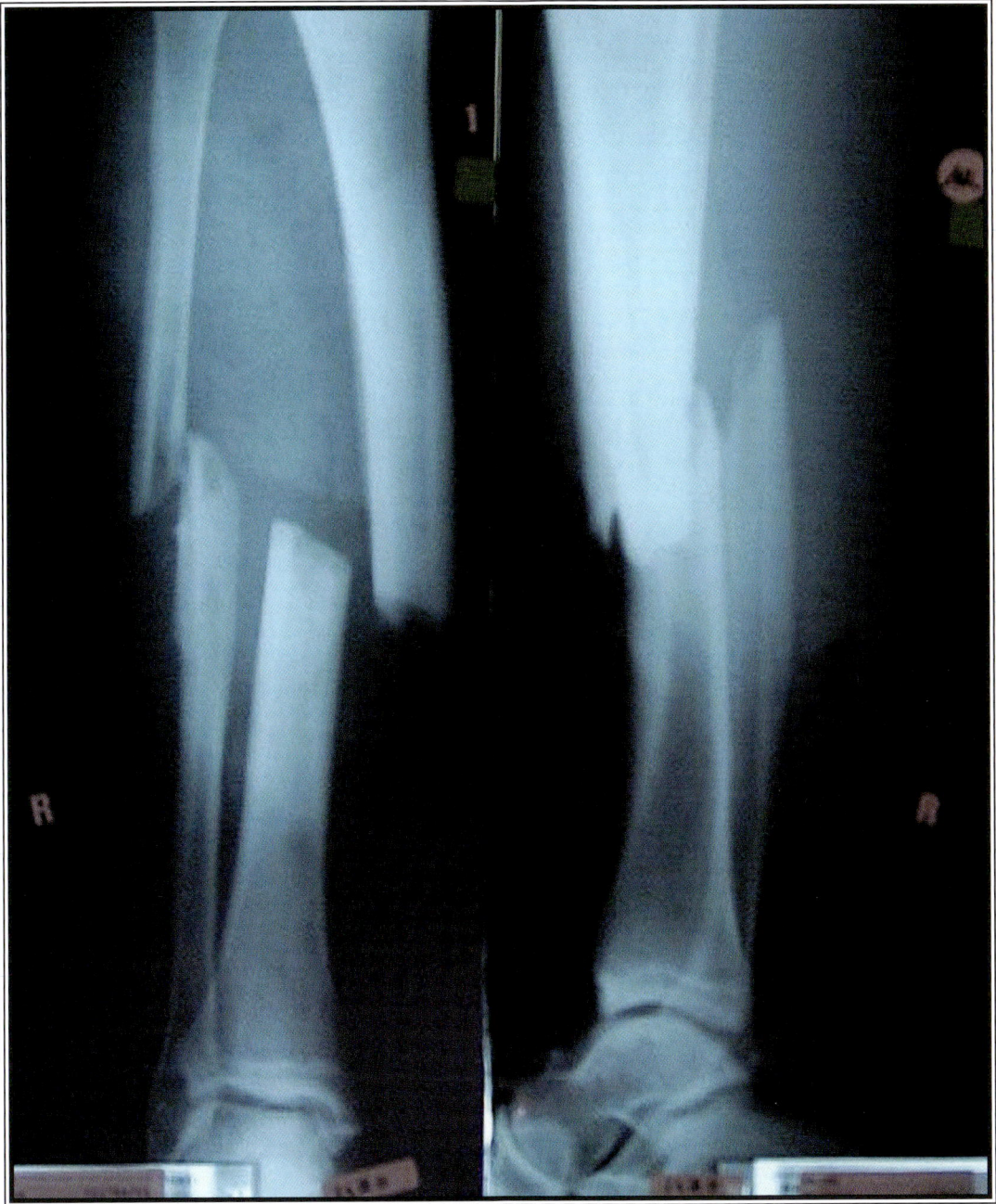

they belong. After the bone is reset, it will "knit" itself back together and become strong again. ～ Doctors help fix badly broken bones in different ways. Sometimes doctors put casts on broken arms or legs. Other times, they use steel pins or plates to mend broken bones. They do this because bones must be kept from moving around in order to heal the right way. ～ By eating right and getting enough exercise, we can keep the bones of our skeletal system healthy. Having healthy bones means

Newborn babies have about 300 bones. Their soft bones fuse together and harden as they grow older.

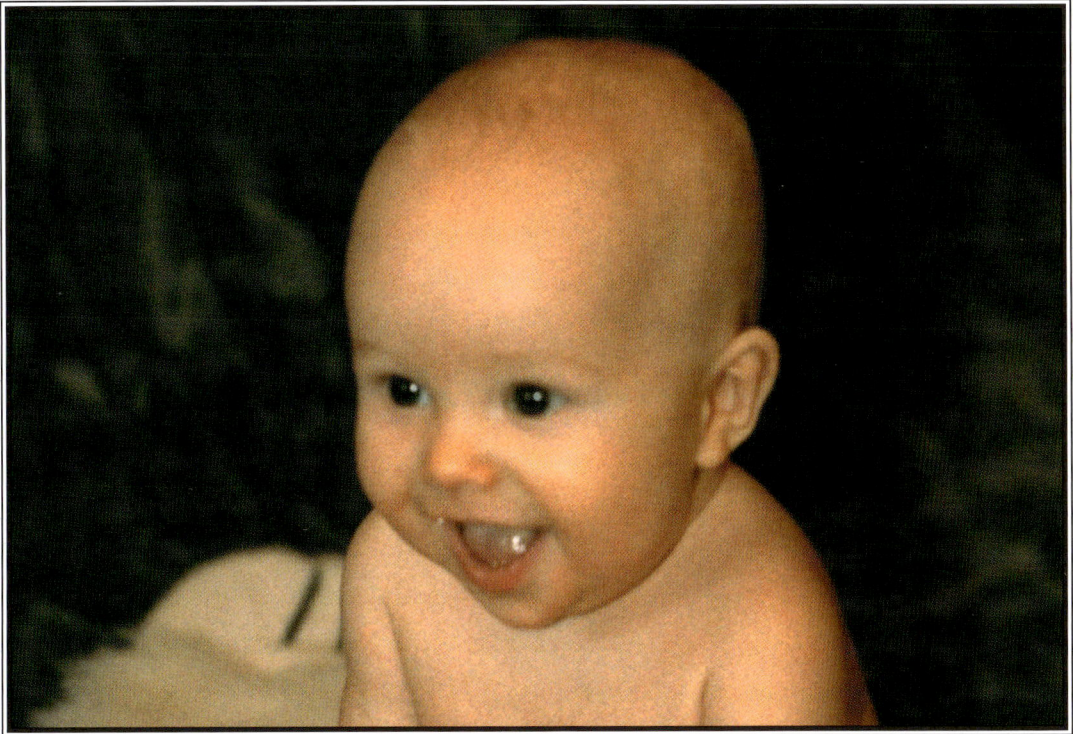

that we can move our bodies in any way we need to enjoy

an active life.

A baby's bones are soft at first but become hard

Body Support

Skeletons give our bodies support and structure. This activity will show you how the bones of the skeletal system make our bodies sturdier.

What You Need

Modeling clay or Play-Doh*
Straws or sticks

What You Do

1. Make a model of an ostrich out of some of the clay. Give the ostrich long legs and a long neck.
2. Try to make your ostrich stand up. Is it wobbly? Is it falling apart?
3. Now make another model ostrich, but this time use the straws or sticks as "bones" and form the clay around them. Is your ostrich able to stand? Is it more or less wobbly than before? How did adding a skeleton change the ostrich?

* Play-Doh is a registered trademark of Hasbro, Incorporated

H A N D S   O N

The skeletons of these fish show through their skin

INFORMATION

Index

Words to Know

blood clot (BLUD klot)—a thickening of blood that forms a plug

cells (SELLZ)—the tiny building blocks that make up all living things

organs (OR-genz)—parts of the body with a particular job, such as the lungs, stomach, and eyes

oxygen (AHK-si-jen)—an invisible gas in the air that people and animals must breathe to live

spinal cord (SPY-nul kord)—a thick band of fibers that runs from the brain throughout the body

Read More

Balestrino, Philip. *The Skeleton Inside You.* New York: HarperCollins Children's Books, 1991.

Gilbert, Laura. *The Skeletal System.* New York: The Rosen Publishing Group, 2001.

Simon, Seymour. *Bones: Our Skeletal System.* New York: Morrow Junior Books, 1998.

Internet Sites

The Discovery Channel:
discoverykids.com
http://yucky.kids.discovery.com/
noflash/body/pg000124.html

Indianapolis Marion County Public
Library InfoZone
http://infozone.imcpl.org/kids_skel.htm

Minnesota State University EMuseum
http://emuseum.mnsu.edu/biology/hum
ananatomy/skeletal/skeletalsystem.html